P9-DLZ-622

by **Dan Gutman**

paintings by
Steve Johnson and **Lou Fancher**

HarperCollins*Publishers*

In memory of Harold Berlin
—D.G.

To our parents,
who taught us to keep our eyes on the ball
—S.J. and L.F.

Casey Back at Bat

Manufactured in China.

For information address HarperCollins Children's Books, a division of HarperCollins Publishers, 1350 Avenue of the Americas, New York, NY 10019.
www.harpercollinschildrens.com

Library of Congress Cataloging-in-Publication Data is available.
ISBN-10: 0-06-056025-8 — ISBN-13: 978-0-06-056025-6
ISBN-10: 0-06-056026-6 (lib. bdg.) — ISBN-13: 978-0-06-056026-3 (lib. bdg.)

Design by Lou Fancher
1 2 3 4 5 6 7 8 9 10
First Edition

I'm sure you've heard of Casey, the baseball world sensation,
whose famous strikeout lost a game and stunned a hopeful nation.
Well, if you think *that* tale was sad, sit down, let's have a chat,
and I'll tell you all a story I call *Casey Back at Bat*.

'Twas the last game of the season, with Mudville tied for first.
The players fought all summer; for a pennant they did thirst.

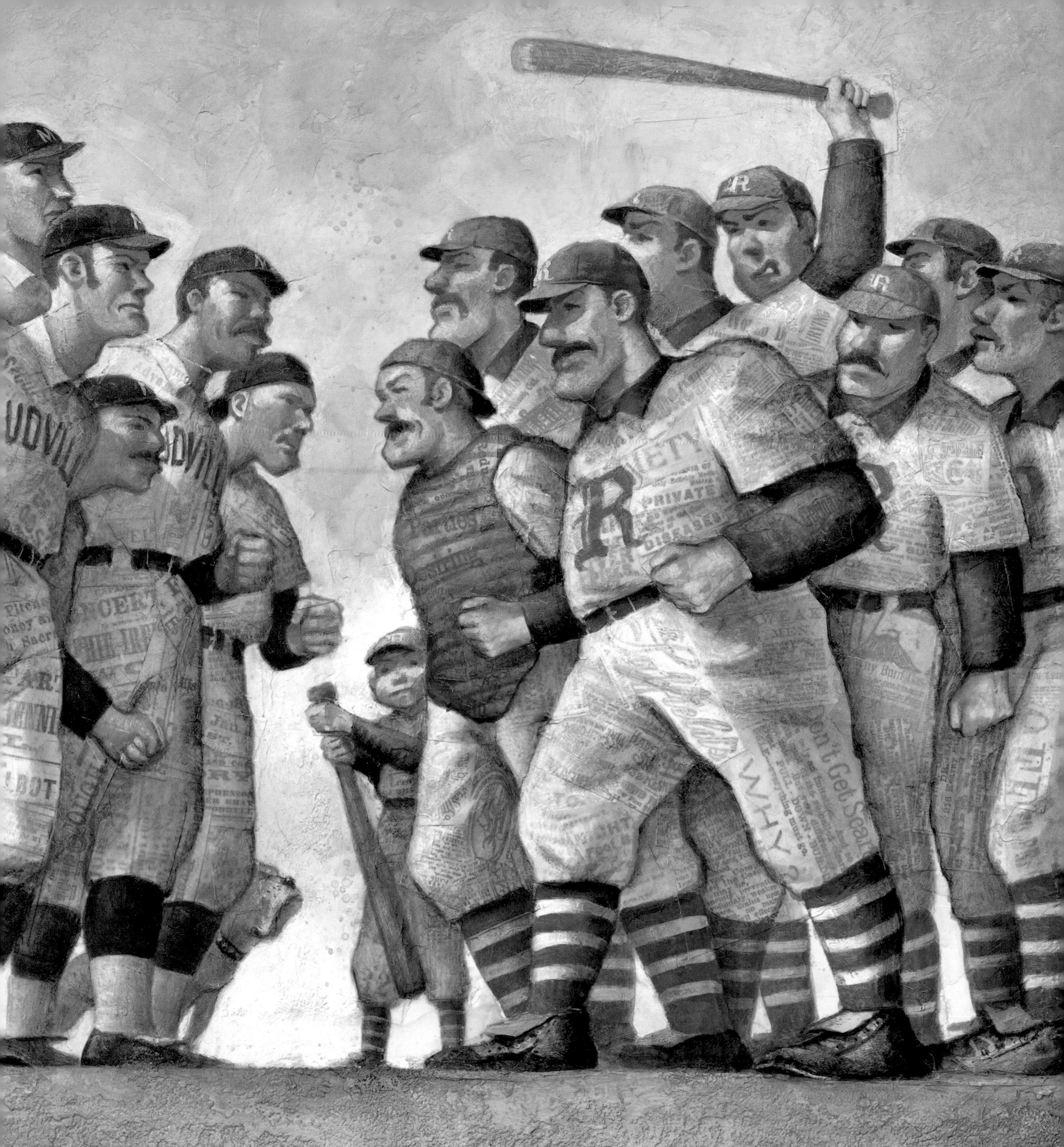

But Rutland shared the lead as well; the teams stood face-to-face.
To the victor—fame and fortune. To the loser—second place.

With Mudville down three runs to one, it was the final inning.
Two men were on, but two were out. There seemed no hope of winning.
Yet they would not surrender. Their motto—"Never quit!"
Mighty Casey grabbed his bat. It was his turn to hit.

MUDVILLE
MUDVILLE
BROS.
Sole Agents
PALACE HOTEL
CANADIAN PACIFIC

His arms, his legs, his neck, his lips–his *teeth* had muscles too.
They rippled from his little toe up to his eyes of blue.
He sneered, he snarled at Mudville's foes, then threw the fans a smirk.
Some ladies found him handsome. Some thought he was a jerk.

CLEANSE
Your Blood
CULVERS
Sarsaparilla

The pitcher hurled his fastball—a perfect strike, and then a fan yelled out, "Hey, Casey! Are you gonna whiff again?"

The runners took their places. Once more the pitcher threw.
He nipped the outside corner. The ump cried out,

"Strike two!"

Again the pitcher gripped the ball and gave a forceful fling.
Casey brought his bat back and decided he would swing.

He swung so hard it sliced the air. It echoed, then it cracked,
when much to everyone's surprise . . . the ball our hero whacked!

"That shot might go five hundred feet!" one bleacher creature reckoned.
"I showed 'em!" cackled Casey as he rounded first and second.
The Mudville fans began to cheer, a roar that started growing
as they watched the ball go o'er the wall,

and then... it kept on going!

It soared by hills and valleys, ever higher in the sky,
past houses, farms, and villages, so swiftly did it fly.
It crossed the great Atlantic, where it almost struck a bird,
but Casey didn't have a clue, for he was roundin' third.

In Italy an artist thought he'd made his masterpiece,

with a painting of a tower and some flowers and some geese.

He had to start all over when the baseball changed the scene.
(And this, you see, shows perfectly why leaning towers lean.)

In Egypt three small children were engaged in some hijinks,
when a baseball zipping past 'em knocked the nose right off the Sphinx.
It ricocheted to where they played and almost hit those kids,
but instead it zoomed right by them and straight up the pyramids!

In India two rhinos who were lolling in a pond
looked up and saw this baseball flying 'cross the great beyond.

They ate their lunch and snorted, taking time to smack their lips.

They hardly seemed to notice, up until the big eclipse.

It flew so fast it raced through time, some sixty million years,
to when *T. rex* and the stegosaurus roamed the hemispheres.
The creatures were quite terrified, so underground they slinked,
and now you know how dinosaurs, in fact, became extinct.

On The Moon
HOUSTON CHRONICLE
Spacemen Are Home Safe

In the depths of outer space, an astronaut named Janet
shrieked, "Eureka! I have found it! I've discovered a new planet!"
Her partner took a look and told her, "Janet, in your dreams.
I've yet to see a planet sewn together at the seams."

MUDVILLE
HANDICAP
There is a Time and Place
for Everything
Dobbins
Scored.
Knee Pants
Long Pants
BRAG!
BRAG!

Meanwhile, back in Mudville, total strangers hugged and kissed.

Casey crossed the plate and told reporters, "It's all in the wrists!"

He hadn't been this happy since the moment of his birth,

but from the upper atmosphere . . . the ball returned to Earth!

Now Dunn, the center fielder, had already left the ground,
and Neft and White, in left and right, were chatting on the mound.

But Moe, the little shortstop, saw a streak come from above.
He raised his arm in self-defense. The ball plopped in his glove!

Oh, somewhere in this crazy world, some kids are having fun.
Some are telling knock-knock jokes. Some skateboard in the sun.
And somewhere kids eat hot dogs piled up high with sauerkraut,
but there's *still* no joy in Mudville—hard-luck Casey has . . .

flied

OUT.